THE LONG JOURNEY HOME

THE LONG JOURNEY HOME

by David Bedford   illustrated by Penny Ives

Dixie woke up. What was that noise?
There was something crying, *meow, meow* . . .

so he crept through the hole
in the fence to see who it was.

Behind the fence he found a kitten.
"I've lost my mother!" it wailed.

Dixie looked around. "Does she have a stripy tail?"
"Yes!" said the kitten. "And pointy ears."
"Follow me," said Dixie. "I'll take you to her."

"Thank you, Dixie!" said the kitten's mother, but Dixie didn't hear her because . . .

he'd already gone to see who was hopping
up and down among the long grasses.
Boing! Boing! Boing! it went.

"Why are you bouncing?" asked Dixie.
"I can't fly yet," said the baby owl. "And I'm looking for my mother."

Boing!

Boing!

Boing!

"Does she live in the trees?"
asked Dixie.
"Yes, she does," said
the baby owl.
"Then follow me,"
Dixie said.

Boing!

Boing!

Boing!

"Thank you, Dixie!" called the owl's mother, but Dixie didn't hear. He'd already gone farther into the woods to see who was making that terrible noise.

YOW-WOW-WOW-WOWWWWWWWWW

"*YOW!*" cried the fox cub. "I can't find my way home."

"Where do you live?" asked Dixie.

"In the side of a hill," said the fox cub.

"Follow me," said Dixie. "I can see your mother looking for you."

"Thank you, Dixie," said the fox
cub's mother. "But shouldn't you be
home by now? It will soon be dark."
Dixie turned to go, but . . .

which way was home?

Everything looked
different in the dark.

Dixie was lost.

"Don't worry," said the foxes,
"we'll show you where to go."
They led Dixie to the edge of
the woods.
"We don't know the way from
here," said the cubs' mother.
Dixie didn't know the way either.
What was he going to do next?

"Look, Dixie, I can fly now!" called
the baby owl. "Follow us!"
Dixie followed the little owl and his
family through the moonlight, until
he came to the long grass.

"We don't know where to go from here," said the baby owl.

"But we do," squeaked a small voice. "Come with us."

Dixie followed the
kitten and his mother
through the tunnels
in the grass until . . .

he knew exactly where he was! There was
the hole in the fence, and there, on the
other side, someone was waiting for him.

"I've been looking for you everywhere!" said Dixie's mother. "You shouldn't have gone out on your own in the dark. You could have got lost."

Dixie was happy to be home.

For Annie, Eva, Dan, and Dixie
~DB

For Aaron and Isaac
~PI

First U.S. edition published in 2002.

Text copyright © 2001 by David Bedford.
Illustrations copyright © 2001 by Penny Ives.

Published by Troll Communications L.L.C.

Published by arrangement with Little Tiger Press, London.

ISBN 0-8167-7456-0

Printed in the United States of America.

10 9 8 7 6 5 4 3 2